MOSES IN THE BULRUSHES

Once, long ago, there was a cruel of Egypt who ordered the death

of all Hebrew s. The

said that the s must be drowned

in the River Nile.

Now there was one Hebrew

who gave birth to a .

"How can I let the take my

 ?" she said to her little .

"I will hide him."

The brave managed to hide

her from the

for three months. When her

was too old to hide she said to her

little , "Bring me some

from the river and I will make a

 for him."

The little watched her

 weave a for the .

It looked like a cradle. "I will make

the water-tight so that it will

float in the river among the ,"

her said. And she set to work.

Early the next morning, when there was

nobody about, the Hebrew

carried the with her in

it to the river. She put it in among the

tall at the water's edge.

"You must stay close by and keep

watch," she told her little .

The little sat down not very

far away from where the was

floating in the water among the .

After a time the young from

the came down to the river to

bathe. With her were some of her
 .

When the spied the among the she sent one of her

 to fetch it out of the water.

As soon as the saw the

handsome lying in the ,

she said "He must be one of the

Hebrew s that my father, the
, wishes dead!" One of her

took the in her arms and the

 said, "We must save him!"

This was all the little

needed to hear. She ran to the

and asked her if she would like to hire

a nurse for the .

"I know a Hebrew nurse who will

take good care of the ," the

little said eagerly.

"Bring her here," said the ,

"and I will hire her to take care of the

 in her own home."

The little ran all the way home

to tell her the wonderful

news.

"The 's daughter, the

 , found our ," she told

her . "Come at once. She is going

to hire you to be his nurse."

The brave did not dare look

at her precious as she knelt

before the smiling .

"You must take good care of this

 ," the told her, "until he

can come and live in the with me."

"I will be like a to him, your

Highness," said the new nurse, with a

happy smile.

"Call him Moses," the went

on, "for the word Moses means drawn

out of the water..."

Moses was now safe from the Egyptian 's fierce for it soon became known that the was taking care of him. She did not have any idea that the Hebrew nurse she had hired was really the of the . Sometimes the came with her to visit the .

she had adopted, and to have a word

with the and give her money.

After a few years the sent for

Moses. In the magnificent

he was treated like a young prince. He

had beautiful clothes to wear and a

clever to help him learn. He

had plenty of toys to play with and a

 to ride.

But one of the things Moses liked to

do best was to wander through the

wonderful gardens looking at

the flowers and birds.

When Moses grew up he left the

court of the . He was never

to return to the , for by now he

had made an enemy of the .

After many years, Moses became the

leader of his own people, the Hebrews.

He promised to lead them to a rich

land where they could settle in peace.